FACES
ONLY A MOTHER
COULD LOVE

Jennifer Owings Dewey

Boyds Mills Press

For my mother

Thanks to
Yongtae Kim-Henry and Elliot
for page 32

Published by Caroline House
Boyds Mills Press, Inc.
A Highlights Company
815 Church Street
Honesdale, Pennsylvania 18431
Printed in Mexico

Publisher Cataloging-in-Publication Data
Dewey, Jennifer Owings.
    Faces only a mother could love / written and illustrated by
Jennifer Owings Dewey.—1st ed.
[32]p. : col. ill. ; cm.
Summary : With full-color realistic illustrations this picture book
explores the world of unusual baby animals.
ISBN 1-56397-046-5
1. Wild animals—Infancy—Juvenile literature. 2. Animals—Infancy—
Pictorial works—Juvenile literature. [Wild animals—Infancy. 2.
Animals—Infancy—Pictorial works.] I. Title.
591.3 / 9—dc20   1996   AC
Library of Congress Catalog Card Number 95-76353

First edition, 1996
Book designed by Jean Krulis
The text of this book is set in 16-point Galliard.
The illustrations are done in color pencil.
Distributed by St. Martin's Press

10 9 8 7 6 5 4 3 2 1

Contents

Japanese macaque monkey   7

Chimpanzee   7

Tarsier   9

Rhinoceros   11

Giant anteater   12

Pelican   15

Great horned owl   16

Sloth   19

Manatee   21

Hognose snake   22

Jackson's chameleon   24

Hawaiian tree snail   26

Frog   28

Sphinx moth caterpillar   30

Paper wasp   30

Human mother and child   32

Babies are beautiful. Right? Wrong! Babies are usually beautiful in their own mother's eyes, but they often look bizarre and strange to others.

In the following pages are some especially odd-looking babies. They are animals whose faces I find fascinating. They are faces only a mother could love . . . .

Japanese macaque monkey

A Japanese macaque monkey's face is pinched and wrinkled, with big brown eyes. From the moment the baby is born, it stays close to its mother. The baby presses its face against its mother's chest for comfort. Mother and baby spend long hours together, looking into each other's faces.

By touching her baby and looking into its face, the mother helps form a bond that lasts a lifetime. Father monkeys stay at a distance, keeping a lookout for danger. Their warning calls give mothers time to snatch up their young and run for cover.

Chimpanzee

Chimpanzee faces resemble human faces. Chimps are primates, closely related to human beings. Many of their expressions show feelings we understand. When we look at a young chimpanzee's face, we can imagine that it feels surprise, excitement, or anger.

Tarsier

The tiny, furry tarsier mother is only as big as a chipmunk, but has eyes that seem to fill up her face. Her baby could fit neatly into a tablespoon when it is first born. Like the mother, the baby tarsier has huge eyes. Tarsiers live in the rain forest and hunt for insects at night. Their large eyes help them see in the dark.

Tarsiers are related to primates. The female has one baby at a time and raises it herself. The baby clings to its mother's chest for the first weeks of life and dares not let go. If it loses its grip, the baby would tumble to the forest floor.

The tarsier mother is watchful and protective of her little one. Even when she is resting, she keeps one eye partly open, on the lookout for danger.

Rhinoceros

The newborn rhinoceros has a face very like its mother's, with bumpy, creased skin, tiny eyes, and small flaps over its ears. But the baby rhino does not have a horn. The horn, made of tightly packed hair, comes later.

A baby rhinoceros is called a calf. It depends on its mother's protection and will follow her everywhere. When the calf is three or four years old, the mother may have a new baby, and the calf will be on its own.

Rhinoceroses do not see well. They rely on their senses of smell and hearing to avoid danger and to find water in the dry African countryside where they live.

The mother rhino will charge at her enemies, holding her powerful, horned head close to the ground and grunting and snorting with rage. Unless it is close to breeding time, the mother rhino will drive away all males, even the calf's father.

Giant anteater

A giant anteater baby has a long nose covered with hair, just like its parents. It has brown eyes with heavy lids and thick lashes. Although the baby anteater looks the same as an adult anteater, the baby doesn't yet know how to use its nose for poking into ant nests and termite mounds.

For the first six weeks of life, the anteater baby rides around on its mother's back, clinging to her coat and feeding on her warm milk.

A grown-up giant anteater is six feet long from the tip of its nose to the end of its tail. It has sharp claws to help break apart termite mounds or dig in the ground for ants.

Giant anteaters are found in Central and South America. They live on a diet of insects, which dart in many directions trying to get away from the anteater's two-foot-long sticky tongue.

Pelican

When a baby pelican, or chick, hatches from an egg, it has a bald head and bags under its eyes. Its pouch is a dull brown color, not bright orange like its mother's.

A mother pelican is in charge of her chicks, keeping them warm, safe, and well-fed in a nest at the water's edge. Her deep pouch makes it easier to bring back enough fish for all her young.

When the chicks are able to fly, they soar over the water with their mother. Pelicans hunt together, watching the surface of the water for schools of silvery fish to scoop into their pouches.

Great horned owl

Great horned owlets hatch from their eggs by cracking open the shells with sharp, hooked beaks. They have huge eyes that are open and staring.

A mother great horned owl works very hard to keep her chicks fed. She makes constant trips away from the nest, coming back with fat rodents that she cuts into bits so each growing owlet can have its share.

Most owls hunt at night. Their large eyes help them search for food in the dark. The feathers on a great horned owl's face grow in a pattern that helps absorb sound. Great horned owls can hear even the faint scampering of mice on the ground.

Sloth

Mother sloth and baby might be twins from the look of their faces, with eyes that are dark and spaced widely apart.

A baby sloth licks its mother's mouth and chin with a red, wet tongue and tastes the leftover bits of leaves its mother has chewed. In this way it learns which leaves are safe to eat.

A mother sloth has one baby a year. She raises each one alone, keeping it with her for six months. When it is time to breed again, the baby stays behind in the tree where it was raised, and the mother goes off to find a new home with her new baby.

Sloths do everything slowly. They hang so still in the trees that insects such as mites, ticks, and beetles set up housekeeping in the sloth's thick coat.

Manatee

A young manatee cruises slowly through the water. It has a pudgy, lumpy face and tiny eyes. The baby manatee, called a calf, presses its face against its mother's skin, gaining reassurance from her closeness.

The baby manatee is born under water and then pushed to the surface by its mother so it can breathe. Even though these cowlike animals live in water, they have lungs like humans and must breathe air to survive.

Manatees have thick, wrinkled hides that are very sensitive to touch. They like to rub and bump against each other. Manatee calves roll and play together, squealing with pleasure.

A calf nurses from its mother for several months. It may go on nursing from time to time, even after it has learned to graze on underwater plants. The calves grow slowly. At birth they weigh about fifty pounds; at full size they may weigh up to two thousand pounds.

Hognose snake

Hognose snakes get their name from their noses, which look a little like the noses on hogs.

Like many reptiles, hognose snake babies hatch from leathery eggs with their eyes wide open. Within a few hours they slither off and begin life on their own. Their mother may never see them. After she has left her eggs in a secure, warm place, the mother hognose does not stay around to see them hatch.

Jackson's chameleon

The knobby, bumpy skin on a baby chameleon's face helps it to blend in with the leaves and vines of the jungle where it lives. When the little chameleon is grown up, it will have three horns on its face. The horns are made of tough skin that grows out of its hard, bony skull.

A Jackson's chameleon has eyes that swivel in the sockets. This is useful when the animal sits absolutely still, trying to remain invisible to enemies. Without moving any part of its body, the chameleon is able to keep watch with its revolving eyes.

A big danger for chameleons is other chameleons. Little ones often become meals for bigger ones. These creatures are unfriendly to one another by nature.

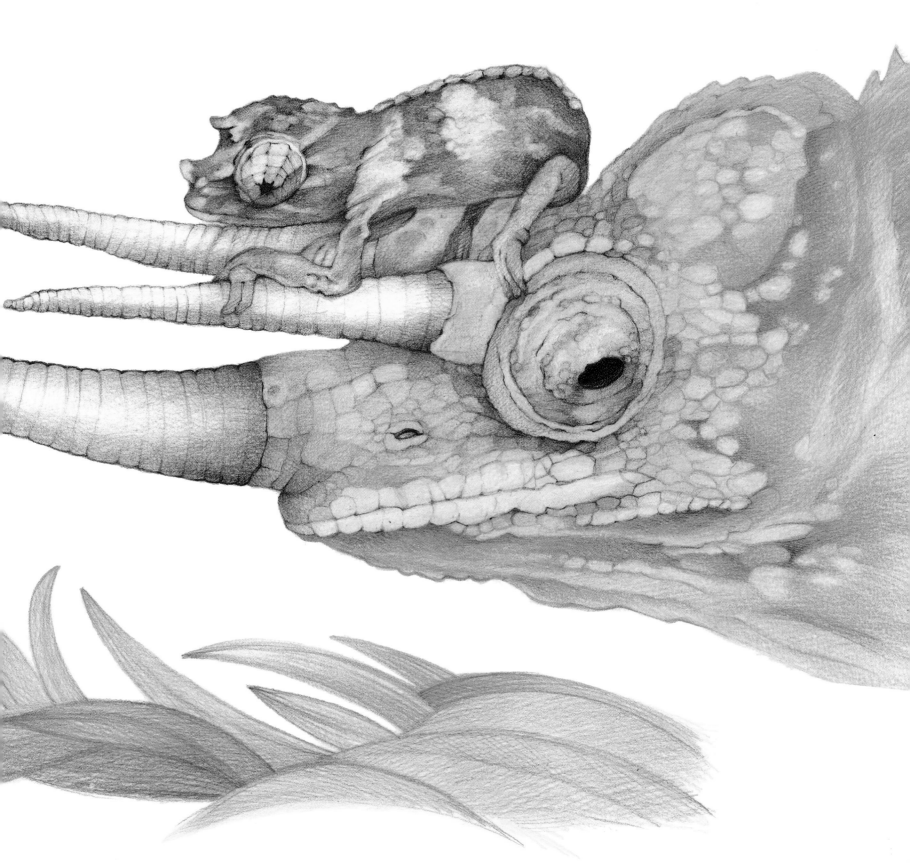

Hawaiian tree snail

A tiny, slippery snail baby with a pale wet face hatches from an egg. The baby snail's eyes are black dots on the tips of the stalks on its face. A baby snail is identical to its mother and father, only smaller.

Most baby snails creep away from their egg case right after hatching, independent from the start. But the Hawaiian tree snail baby is sheltered and protected by a clutch of adult snails while it grows up. It lives in colonies with others of its kind. Living in groups helps to ensure that more baby snails will survive to adulthood.

Frog

A frog mother may hide her bundle of eggs under a lily pad or carry the eggs in a packet of slime on her back. Frogs have many different ways of sheltering their eggs. Some species of frogs hold their eggs inside their mouths, releasing them when the eggs are ready to hatch. But frog mothers never see the faces of their babies.

Freshly hatched tadpoles are the favorite food of fish, other frogs, birds, and salamanders. The tadpoles who grow quickly have the best chance of survival. Some tadpoles take up to two weeks to grow into true frogs. But for others, "childhood" lasts only two or three days. Slippery little pre-frogs develop eyes, mouths, feet, legs, and loud croaking voices.

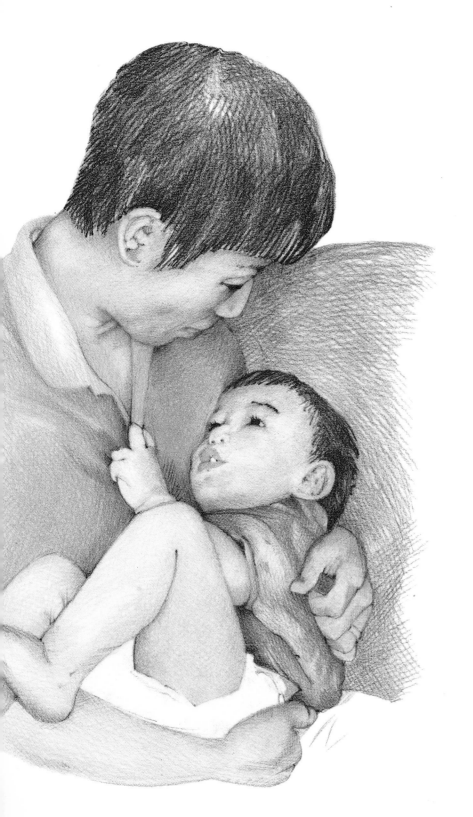

Human mother and baby

A sleepy baby rests easily on his mother's shoulder. With his soft face pressed close, he feels secure. The contact he has with his mother helps to make him feel strong and self-assured.

It is through looking, touching, and feeding that a mother comes to know her child and the child comes to trust his mother. This connection can hold them together in the years it takes for the child to grow and learn the lessons of life.

Sphinx moth caterpillar

The face visible on the brown Sphinx moth caterpillar is a pretend face. The real face is at the other end of the caterpillar's body. The false face fools predators that might want to eat the caterpillar. They see a scary face and pass by.

Many insects in their developing stages protect themselves by changing colors or growing cocoons. Others wear disguises, like the Sphinx moth caterpillar does.

Paper wasp

The female paper wasp works hard to raise her young. The mother's face is made up of antennae, eyes, and a big, strong jaw. She uses her jaw to chew up wood shavings, then mixes these with saliva from inside her mouth. With this paste she builds a nest for her eggs.

Young wasps have faces like their mother, only smaller. When the mother's work is done and the young are grown, the mother dies. It becomes the task of the new generation to build more nests and lay eggs.

FACES ONLY A MOTHER COULD LOVE

Jennifer Owings Dewey

Boyds Mills Press

For my mother

Thanks to
Yongtae Kim-Henry and Elliot
for page 32

Published by Caroline House
Boyds Mills Press, Inc.
A Highlights Company
815 Church Street
Honesdale, Pennsylvania 18431
Printed in Mexico

Publisher Cataloging-in-Publication Data
Dewey, Jennifer Owings.
    Faces only a mother could love / written and illustrated by
Jennifer Owings Dewey.—1st ed.
[32]p. : col. ill. ; cm.
Summary : With full-color realistic illustrations this picture book
explores the world of unusual baby animals.
ISBN 1-56397-046-5
1. Wild animals—Infancy—Juvenile literature. 2. Animals—Infancy—
Pictorial works—Juvenile literature. [Wild animals—Infancy. 2.
Animals—Infancy—Pictorial works.] I. Title.
591.3 / 9—dc20   1996   AC
Library of Congress Catalog Card Number 95-76353

First edition, 1996
Book designed by Jean Krulis
The text of this book is set in 16-point Galliard.
The illustrations are done in color pencil.
Distributed by St. Martin's Press

10 9 8 7 6 5 4 3 2 1